January Joker

A strange yellow light filled the back-yard. The snow and the barn had turned yellow.

"See, I told you!" Bradley said. He stepped out onto the porch. Brian, Nate, and Lucy followed him.

Next to the barn, two small creatures hopped around in the middle of a big circle in the snow. They looked like broccoli spears. They had large heads, short arms, and tiny legs.

"Aliens!" said Bradley.

Calendar MYSTERIES

January Joker

by **Ron Roy**

illustrated by
John Steven Gurney

A STEPPING STONE BOOK™

Random House New York

To my niece, Desiree Roy
—R.R.

To Rhys, Issac, and Connor
—J.S.G.

This is a work of fiction. Names, characters, places, and incidents either are the product of the author's imagination or are used fictitiously. Any resemblance to actual persons, living or dead, events, or locales is entirely coincidental.

Text copyright © 2009 by Ron Roy
Illustrations and map copyright © 2009 by John Steven Gurney

www.ronroy.com
www.randomhouse.com/kids

Educators and librarians, for a variety of teaching tools, visit us at
www.randomhouse.com/teachers

Library of Congress Cataloging-in-Publication Data
Roy, Ron.
January joker / by Ron Roy ; illustrated by John Steven Gurney. — 1st ed.
   p.   cm. — (Calendar mysteries) "A Stepping Stone Book."
Summary: Seven-year-olds Bradley, Brian, Nate, and Lucy make observations and gather clues that convince them that their older siblings, cousin, and animals have been captured by hungry space aliens.
ISBN 978-0-375-85661-7 (pbk.) — ISBN 978-0-375-95661-4 (lib. bdg.)
[1. Mystery and detective stories. 2. Extraterrestrial beings—Fiction. 3. Twins—Fiction. 4. Brothers and sisters—Fiction. 5. Cousins—Fiction. 6. Practical Jokes—Fiction.]
I. Gurney, John Steven, ill. II. Title.
PZ7.R8139Jan 2009 [Fic]—dc22   2008016534

Printed in the United States of America

10 9 8 7 6 5 4 3 2

Contents

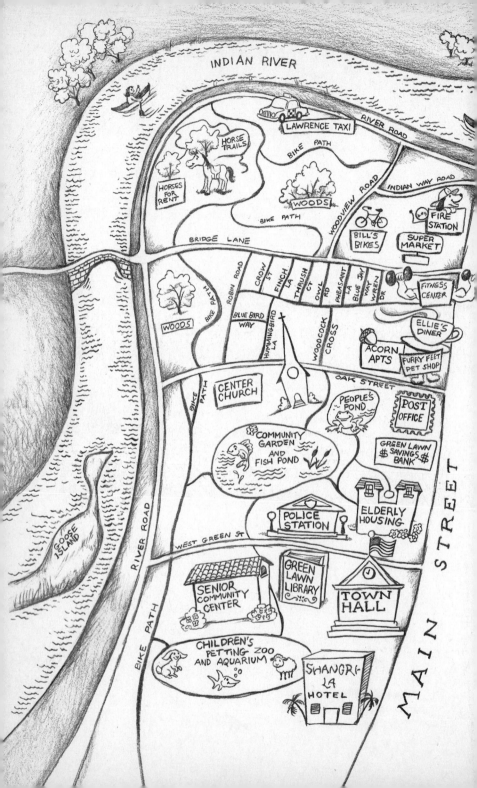

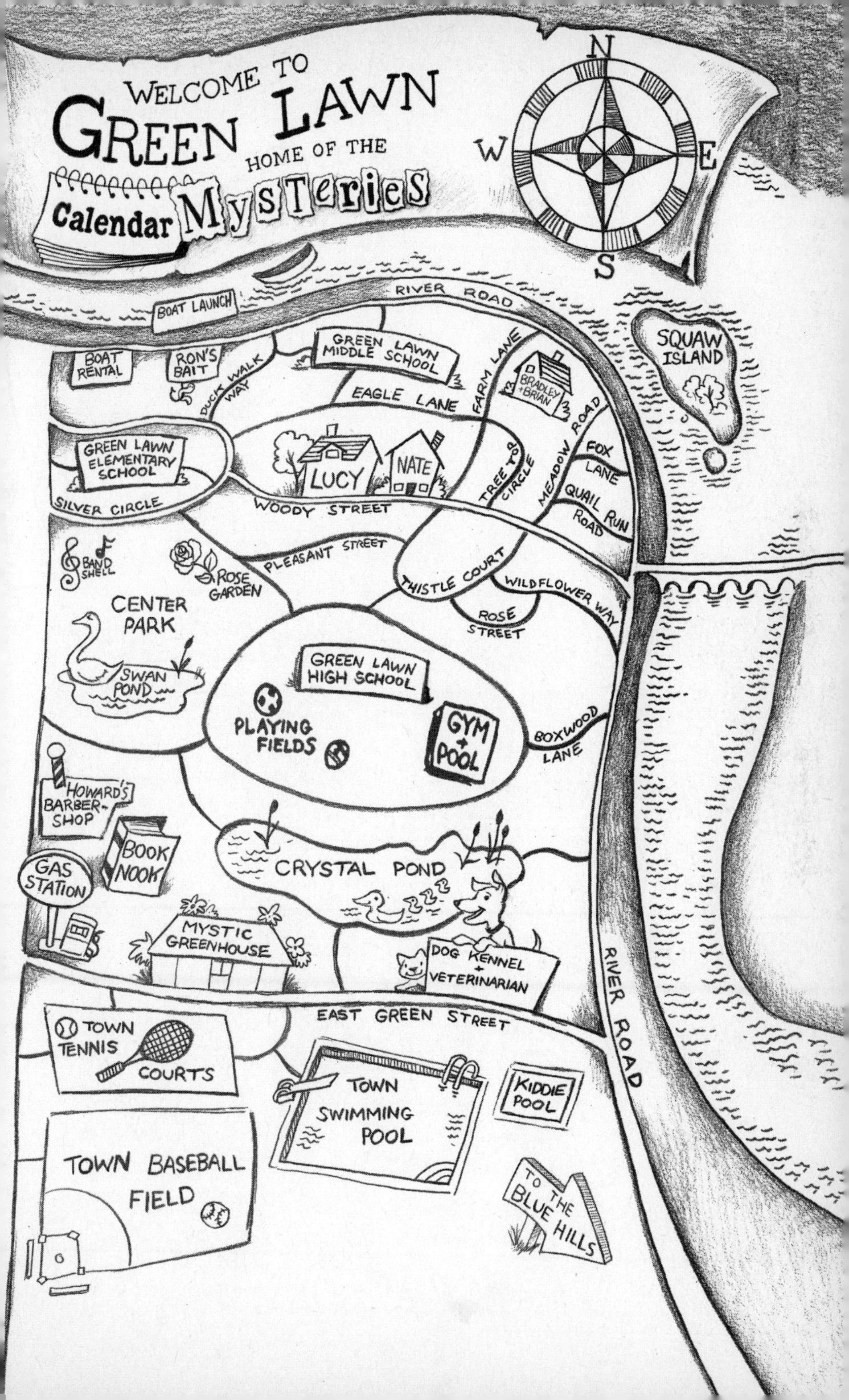

WELCOME TO
GREEN LAWN
HOME OF THE
Calendar Mysteries
N
W
E
S
BOAT LAUNCH
RIVER ROAD
BOAT RENTAL
RON'S BAIT
DUCK WALK WAY
GREEN LAWN MIDDLE SCHOOL
FARM LANE
BRADLEY + BRIAN
EAGLE LANE
SQUAW ISLAND
MEADOW ROAD
GREEN LAWN ELEMENTARY SCHOOL
LUCY
NATE
TREE TOP CIRCLE
FOX LANE
QUAIL RUN ROAD
SILVER CIRCLE
WOODY STREET
PLEASANT STREET
BAND SHELL
ROSE GARDEN
THISTLE COURT
WILDFLOWER WAY
ROSE STREET
CENTER PARK
SWAN POND
GREEN LAWN HIGH SCHOOL
PLAYING FIELDS
GYM + POOL
BOXWOOD LANE
HOWARD'S BARBER-SHOP
BOOK NOOK
GAS STATION
CRYSTAL POND
MYSTIC GREENHOUSE
DOG KENNEL + VETERINARIAN
RIVER ROAD
EAST GREEN STREET
TOWN TENNIS COURTS
TOWN SWIMMING POOL
KIDDIE POOL
TOWN BASEBALL FIELD
TO THE BLUE HILLS

1
Spooky Lights

Bradley Pinto sat up in bed. His red hair was flat on one side. He blinked and rubbed his sleepy brown eyes.

Bradley thought he'd heard a strange noise outside his bedroom. Yawning, he climbed out of bed. He tiptoed by his twin brother's bed. He stepped over the two lumpy sleeping bags on the floor.

Bradley put his ear to the door. No noises. He opened the door. Nothing out there.

Then he noticed a bright light outside his bedroom window.

"Oh my gosh!" he said.

Bradley ran to his brother's bed.

"Hey, Brian. Wake up!" Bradley whispered.

"Umph," Brian mumbled.

Bradley poked Brian's leg. "Bri, wake up! There are weird lights in the backyard!"

A sleeping bag sat up. Inside it was Nate Hathaway, one of Bradley's best friends. "Let me see!" Nate said. He crawled out of his bag. Nate had black hair, like his sister, Ruth Rose. The twins' older brother, Josh, was best friends with Ruth Rose and her neighbor Dink Duncan.

The other sleeping bag popped up. It was Lucy Armstrong. She was Dink's cousin, visiting for a year from California. Her parents were helping build a school on a reservation in Arizona.

"What's going on?" Lucy asked. Her

blond hair was tied in pigtails. She wore
Wonder Woman pajamas.

Brian grinned from his bed. "Bradley
is having a dream," he said.

"I am not!" Bradley said. "There's
something out there, and I'm going to
see what it is!"

Bradley put on his slippers and
stepped out into the dark hallway.

"Wait for us!" Nate said behind him.

The four kids tiptoed through the
house and down into the kitchen.
Bradley pulled open the back door.

A strange yellow light filled the
backyard. The snow and the barn had
turned yellow.

"See, I told you!" Bradley said. He
stepped out onto the porch. Brian, Nate,
and Lucy followed him.

"What is it?" Lucy whispered.

"It's cold out here!" Brian com-
plained.

"Oh my gosh, look!" Nate squealed.

Next to the barn, two small creatures hopped around in the middle of a big circle in the snow. They looked like broccoli spears. They had large heads, short arms, and tiny legs.

"Aliens!" said Bradley.

"What are they doing?" Nate asked.

"J-jumping up and down to get warm!" Brian said. "I can see my breath!"

"Are they really aliens?" Lucy asked.

Nate giggled. "They sure aren't raccoons," he said.

"They're definitely aliens," Bradley said. "I saw pictures just like them in my space book." Bradley had gotten *UFOs and You* for Christmas.

"What's that circle in the snow?" Nate asked.

"It must be where their spaceship landed," Bradley said.

Brian snorted. "Brad, you'll believe anything," he said.

"Well, what do *you* think they are?" Bradley asked.

"I think Nate is pulling another practical joke," Brian said.

"Me?" Nate squeaked.

"Yeah, you," Lucy said. "Like last week when you sent Dink, Josh, and Ruth Rose postcards telling them they'd won a million dollars."

Nate giggled. "Boy, they were mad when they found out it wasn't true," he said.

All four kids laughed.

"So how did you do it?" Brian asked Nate. "How'd you make those two little guys and the circle in the snow, and that yellow light?"

"But I didn't do it!" Nate insisted.

Suddenly the light in the yard went out. The two creatures disappeared in the darkness. There were just the dark barn and the moon on the snow.

"Where did they go?" Bradley asked.

"Ask Nate," Brian said. He turned around and went back inside.

"I'm innocent!" Nate said. He followed Brian into the warm kitchen.

"Let's go in, Bradley," Lucy said. "I'm shivering!"

Bradley watched the empty backyard for another few minutes. He didn't see the light or the aliens again.

"Come back," he whispered. "Please come back."

2
Circle in the Snow

The next morning, Bradley beat Brian to the table. They were dressed alike in warm shirts and jeans. Nate and Lucy came down the stairs next. They wore snow pants, sweaters, and boots.

Dink, Josh, and Ruth Rose were making breakfast. Josh's dog, Pal, was under the table, chewing his favorite toy, a rubber hot dog.

Brian and Bradley's parents rushed into the room. They pulled on coats and hats.

"Dad and I are meeting Dink's and Ruth Rose's parents for breakfast," said Bradley's mother. "We'll be back in a couple of hours. Josh, Dink, and Ruth Rose are in charge."

"I saw space aliens in the backyard last night!" Bradley told his parents.

"That's nice, dear," his mother said. "Tell me all about it when we get back, but now we have to scoot."

"You younger kids listen to the big kids," Bradley's father added.

"We don't need babysitters!" Brian said.

Brian and Bradley, Lucy, and Nate were all in first grade. The three older kids were in sixth.

"Yes, you do," his mother said. "Bye-bye!"

Then they were gone. Just the seven kids and Pal were left in the kitchen.

"Chow time," Josh said. He and Dink

and Ruth Rose brought pancakes, syrup, and glasses of milk to the table.

"Did you see lights in the backyard last night?" Bradley asked Josh.

"Nope. I was dreaming of surfing in Hawaii," Josh said.

The seven kids gobbled up all the pancakes.

"We cooked, so you have to clean up," Josh told the younger kids.

"I'm not doing any dishes!" Brian yelped.

"Just wipe the table and put your dishes in the sink," Ruth Rose said.

"Then come out and we'll take Polly for some exercise," Josh said.

"Can we ride her?" Lucy asked.

"Sure, we all will," Josh said.

Dink, Josh, and Ruth Rose tugged on their coats and boots and left the house. Pal followed them, carrying his rubber hot dog in his mouth.

Lucy and Nate put everything in the sink. Bradley wet a sponge and wiped the table. "You're supposed to help, Bri," he said.

Brian grinned. "Nope, I'm older than you."

"Yeah, by one minute," Bradley said. He tossed the sponge at his brother.

Brian caught it. "Let's go out," he said. "Maybe Bradley can show us where the spaceship landed last night!"

"I thought you didn't believe me," Bradley said.

"I don't," Brian said.

"A lot of people in California see UFOs," Lucy said.

"See?" Bradley said to his brother. "Come on, I'll prove it."

The four kids grabbed hats and coats and mittens. They clumped down the back porch steps in their snow boots.

Bradley led the way toward a flat

space next to the barn. The other three kids followed him like ducklings.

The snow came up to their ankles. They left bootprints as they trudged across the yard.

Bradley was the first to reach it.

"See, I told you," Bradley said. His breath made puffs in front of his mouth.

The other three kids stopped next to
him.

"Awesome!" Nate cried.

They were looking at a circle in the
snow. It was as big as a swimming pool.

The perfect size for a spaceship.

"You were right," Lucy whispered to
Bradley.

3
Aliens Have Three Toes

"This doesn't prove a spaceship landed here," Brian said. "Anything could have made this circle."

"Like what?" Nate asked.

"Um, like kids fooling around on bikes?" Brian offered.

"Then where are the bike tracks?" Bradley asked.

There were no bike tracks.

Just one perfect circle in the snow.

"What are these funny marks?" Lucy asked.

She pointed to a trail of prints. Each print left three small dents in the snow. They led toward the barn.

"Look, there are others, too!" said Bradley.

These were bigger, the size of pancakes.

"Those look like Polly's hoofprints," Brian said. "We'd better go check on her."

The kids ran to the barn. Bradley was the first one inside. He flipped on the light switch.

Polly's stall was empty.

"She's gone!" Bradley said.

Her fresh straw was there.

Her feed and water buckets were full.

But Polly the pony was nowhere to be seen.

"Hey, where are Dink, Josh, and Ruth Rose?" asked Nate.

"Maybe they took Polly for a walk," Lucy suggested to her friends.

Bradley ran to the barn door. "There are no other footprints in the snow," he called. "Just Polly's and those funny pointy ones."

"They must have gone back in the house," Brian said. "Let's go check."

"Bri, they wouldn't take Polly in the house," Bradley said. "Besides, the only footprints are ours. And they're coming *from* the house, not *to* the house."

"Well, I'm checking inside anyway," Brian said. "Kids don't just disappear."

The four kids clumped back up the porch steps. They stomped the snow off their boots. Brian shoved open the door. "Josh?" he yelled.

There was no answer.

The house was silent.

No TV noise, no computer sounds, no video game beeps.

"Where are they?" Nate whispered.

"This is very, very weird," Lucy said.

"They've been taken by the aliens!" Bradley whispered.

Nate giggled.

"Let's try upstairs," Brian said. "I'll bet they're just hiding."

The kids tugged off their boots and followed Brian.

The first room was Josh's. The door was closed. A sign on the door said: NO HUMANS ALLOWED.

"Josh, are you in there?" Bradley called.

No answer.

Brian knocked on the door, then pushed it open.

"Oh my goodness!" Lucy said. "A burglar has been here! Josh's stuff is all messed up!"

The bed was unmade.

Clothes were all over the floor.

"This is how he always keeps his room," Bradley said.

"Josh's computer is on," Brian said. He walked over to his big brother's desk.

"He was on a Web site about UFOs!" Nate said.

Lucy picked up a paper from the tray of the printer. "Uh-oh," she said.

"What?" Brian asked.

Lucy handed him the paper. The others gathered around to read what Josh had printed:

Scientists feel that space aliens have landed on Earth.

In China, sixteen children have disappeared.

In France, farm animals have vanished.

In each case, a large circle was found on the ground. Small, three-pointed footprints were found near the scenes as well.

Dr. Barney Piper is a well-known expert on space. He was asked what he thinks of these strange occurrences:

"I have always known there was life on other planets," Dr. Piper stated. "I think these aliens have run out of food. It is my belief that they are hungry and coming to Earth. They are taking our children and animals back into space to their home planet."

Bradley poked his brother. "That's what I saw last night," he whispered. "The aliens were stealing Polly!"

4
Phone Home

Just then the telephone rang in the hall.

Bradley ran to answer it. "Hello?" he said. "Josh, is that you?"

The other kids hurried over. They pressed their ears close to the phone so they could hear.

"Josh, I can hardly hear you!" Bradley yelled into the phone. "Where are Dink and Ruth Rose?"

"They're here with me!" everyone heard Josh say. "Polly's here, too."

"But where are you?" Bradley asked.

"Aliens got us!" Josh answered. "We're in a spaceship!"

Then the line went dead.

The four kids stared at each other.

Lucy's eyes were as big as meatballs.

Brian was tugging on his red hair.

Nate shook his head. "This has to be a joke," he said.

"Josh sounded far away," Bradley said.

"Wait a minute!" Lucy yelled. "How could he call you from space? Do space-ships have phones?"

"Josh never goes anywhere without his cell phone," Bradley said.

"I still think it's a trick," Nate said. He grabbed the telephone.

"Who are you calling?" Lucy asked.

"Ruth Rose," Nate said. "I saw her put her cell phone in her pocket."

The four kids sat in a circle on the floor. Nate dialed his sister's number.

Everyone leaned toward the phone.

"It's ringing!" Nate whispered.

Then they all heard Ruth Rose's voice. ". . . little people with . . . feet . . . don't know what . . . we're going . . . try call . . . again. . . ."

Then they heard something roaring, then nothing.

"Oh my gosh!" Bradley said. "What should we do?"

Nate started to giggle. "We're home alone!" he said.

"This isn't funny," Lucy said. "And we're not alone. We have each other. Besides, Pal is here."

"He is?" Brian said. "Where?"

"Oh no!" Bradley screeched.

The four kids pounded down the stairs.

They yelled, "PAL! COME, PAL!" as they ran.

"You guys split up and search the

house!" Brian said. "I'll look outside."

Bradley, Nate, and Lucy looked in every corner of the house.

They checked all the closets.

They peeked into kitchen cupboards and under chairs and in the basement and up the chimney.

Pal was gone.

5
Lucy's List

"We have to call the cops!" Nate cried.

"And tell them what?" Brian asked. "They'll just laugh at us."

"We have to do something!" Bradley said. "Everyone is disappearing!"

"Don't panic," Lucy said. "Let's just make a list."

"Ha!" Nate barked. "A list of what?"

"A list of clues," Lucy said.

"Okay, we'll make a list," Brian said. "But you sound just like your cousin Dink."

They sat at the kitchen table.

Bradley gave Lucy a pen and paper from off the counter.

Lucy wrote the word CLUES on the top of the page.

"Okay, what are the clues we've seen so far?" she asked.

"The circle in the snow," Bradley said.

Lucy wrote it down.

"The funny footprints," Nate added. "But I still don't think aliens have invaded Green Lawn."

"Nate, people are vanishing!" said Bradley. "My horse and dog are gone!"

Lucy wrote on her pad. "What else?" she asked.

"I don't believe it, either," Brian said. "But write down that printout we saw next to Josh's computer."

Lucy added to her list.

"The phone calls," Nate said. He

couldn't stop himself from grinning.

"Excellent!" Lucy said. "Okay, here's what we saw: aliens, a circle in the snow, weird footprints, Polly and Pal are gone, the big kids have disappeared. . . ."

Lucy looked up. "This is creepy," she said.

Suddenly they heard a tapping noise.

"They're here!" Bradley whispered.

"Chill out, Brad," Brian said. "It's just a woodpecker . . . or something."

They heard the tapping again.

This time they all looked at the window behind the table.

A green face with big teeth was peering in at them. An instant later, the thing vanished.

"The aliens are back!" screamed Brian.

"Look! There's another one!" Lucy shouted, pointing at the window over the sink. This time the face was yellow.

It had no teeth, but two huge eyes stared in at them. As the kids watched, the figure shot up into the air.

"RUN!" yelled Nate.

The four kids bolted out of their seats. They dashed around the kitchen, bumping into each other.

Finally, they all ended up in the small closet under the stairs.

They huddled together like sardines in a can.

They heard each other's breathing.

"Can you hear them?" Bradley asked.

"Hear them what?" Brian asked.

"I don't know, walking around," Bradley said.

The kids stopped whispering and listened. They heard a clock ticking. The refrigerator motor hummed. A car horn honked in the street.

Nate giggled. "I think I hear them opening the refrigerator."

"Real funny, Nate," Bradley said. "Now do you believe me?"

"I don't want to, but I guess I do," Nate said.

"I might," Brian stated. "Those things were scary-looking!"

"What do you think they want?" Nate asked.

"Easy," Bradley said. "They want us."

"Shut up!" Nate wailed.

"We need a plan," Lucy said calmly.

6
The Plan

"I already have a plan," Nate said. "I'm never leaving this closet."

"Lucy's right," Bradley said. "We can't stay here all morning."

"Why not?" Brian asked. "Mom and Dad will be home in less than an hour."

"Great," said Bradley. "You can be the one to tell them Josh has been kidnapped by space creatures."

"Maybe we could talk to the aliens," Lucy said.

Nate laughed. "Do they speak English?"

"Brad, what does it say about aliens in your UFO book?" Lucy asked.

"Lots of things," Bradley said. "And there are pictures!"

"Where's your book?" Lucy asked.

"In my room, upstairs," Bradley said.

Lucy slowly opened the closet door. She poked her head out and looked around. "I don't see anyone," she whispered to the boys behind her.

Lucy stepped into the hallway.

"Where are you going?" Nate asked.

"I want to see Bradley's book," she said. "I may have an idea."

"Come on, Lucy, I'll show you," Bradley said.

"Wait!" Nate said. "We should lock the doors and pull down all the shades."

The kids tiptoed from room to room, pulling shades and checking locks. Then they followed Bradley upstairs.

His book, *UFOs and You,* lay on the floor.

Bradley opened to a section that showed pictures.

The kids looked at photos of strange creatures.

"Are these real pictures of aliens?" Nate asked.

"The author says they are," Bradley answered.

"But the pictures are fuzzy," Lucy said. "I can't tell what the aliens look like."

"Guys, we saw two looking in the windows," Brian reminded them. "They were disgusting! We have to *do* something!"

Lucy was flipping through Bradley's book. She pointed to a picture of a man standing next to a small creature.

Below was another picture. This one showed strange little tracks in the dirt. Each track had three points.

"Those are exactly like the prints we

saw outside!" Bradley yelled. "I told you guys!"

"Listen," Lucy said. She read a caption under the pictures: "'Dr. Wilfred Ditz says he met several space aliens. He says they were shy and friendly creatures.'"

"Friendly!" Brian squawked. "They're gonna eat our pony!"

"So what's your plan?" Nate asked.

"Those two aliens we saw outside the kitchen might just be hungry," Lucy said.

"Yeah, for some nice juicy first graders!" Brian moaned.

"So what if we feed them?" Lucy continued.

"You mean make them lunch?" Bradley asked.

"Yes," Lucy said. She grinned. "And then we capture them!"

7
The Trade

"Capture them?" Brian squeaked.

"You mean to keep for pets?" Nate asked. "Cool!"

"I'm not touching any aliens!" Brian said. "They could have space cooties!"

"What do we do with them?" Bradley asked.

Lucy closed the book. "We trade them for Dink, Josh, and Ruth Rose," she said. "And Polly and Pal."

The three boys stared at Lucy.

Brian's mouth fell open.

Nate started to laugh.

"I think it's a great idea!" Bradley said.

Nate stopped laughing. "How do you catch an alien?" he asked.

"We leave a trail of food, then trap them," Lucy said.

"We have a skunk trap in the barn!" Bradley said.

"The aliens are too big," Lucy said. Then she grinned. "But we could trap them in that closet!"

"I think this is crazy!" Brian said. "Is this what kids do in California?"

Lucy shook her head. "No, but I saw it in a TV movie," she said. "The kids doing it left some food out. The aliens followed the food right into a closet. Slam! They were caught!"

"Then what happened?" Nate asked with wide eyes.

"I don't know," Lucy said with a

shrug. "My dad made me go to bed."

"Great," Brian said. "We trap some aliens in our closet. Then they breathe fire and burn the house down!"

"They're not dragons," Nate said. "They're just cute little people from another planet."

"Cute little monsters that eat kids and pets," mumbled Brian.

"Let's go check the fridge for bait," Bradley said.

"Any minute now I'm gonna wake up from this dream," Brian said.

The kids followed Bradley to the kitchen. He pulled open the refrigerator door. "Let's see, milk, grapes, cheese, yogurt . . ."

"How about that chocolate cake?" Nate asked.

"No way!" Brian said. "That's for our dessert tonight. I'm not sharing it with any guys from Planet Nutso!"

Lucy pulled out the bowl of green grapes.

"Aliens like grapes?" Nate asked.

Lucy began making a grape trail on the floor. "I don't know," she said. "But maybe green aliens like green food."

Bradley opened the door to the closet under the stairs.

Lucy placed grapes so they led right into the dark space. She put the rest of the grapes inside.

"Now we hide," she said. "If they go in, we lock the door."

The kids hid behind the sofa in the
living room.

"Um, we forgot one thing," Bradley
said.

"What?" Nate asked.

"We locked all the doors," Bradley
said. "How are the aliens supposed to
get in the house?"

"Oops," Lucy said.

She dashed into the kitchen, opened
the door, then ran back.

"Come on, little guys. Come and get
it," Bradley whispered.

"I need to use the bathroom," Brian
announced.

"Shhh," Bradley said. "Aliens have
excellent hearing."

"Brad, I have to go!" Brian said. He
scooted toward the bathroom.

Lucy, Nate, and Bradley waited.

And waited.

The next thing they heard was quiet
footsteps.

8
They Are Listening

"Is that Brian coming back?" Nate whispered.

"I don't know," Bradley said.

Suddenly they all heard a little yelp.

"What was that?" Bradley asked. "Where's Brian?"

They heard a thump.

They heard chewing and swallowing noises.

Then they heard nothing.

The house was silent again.

Nate let out a little giggle. "I guess

they didn't like the grapes, so they took Brian instead!" he said.

"Don't joke around!" Bradley said. "I'm going to look for him!"

"We're coming with you," Lucy whispered.

"We are?" Nate asked.

Lucy nudged him. "We're all in this together!" she said.

The three kids peeked out from behind the sofa. On hands and knees, they crawled into the hallway.

"Look, the bathroom door is open," Bradley said. "Brian's not there!"

"And all the grapes are gone!" Nate said.

It was true. Lucy's trail of grapes had disappeared.

Lucy pointed to the closet door. It was closed.

"I thought we left it open," Nate whispered.

"We did," Lucy whispered back.

Suddenly the hall closet door burst open. Brian jumped out. "Boy, am I glad to see you!" he said. "I thought the green guys got you, too!"

"And we thought they got you!" Bradley said, grinning at his twin.

"They did!" Brian yelled. "I was coming out of the bathroom when something fell over my head! It felt like a hundred little arms grabbed me. They stuck me in the closet!"

"Ugh!" Nate said, pointing to a piece of lint on Brian's shoulder. "Space cooties!"

"Very funny, Nate," Brian said. But he wiped the lint off.

"Did you eat all the grapes I left out?" Lucy asked.

"No, it must have been them," Brian said. "I just ate the ones you put in the closet."

"Did you see the aliens?" Nate asked.

"No!" Brian said. "They threw this over my head!" He reached into the closet and pulled out a fuzzy red cloth.

"That's what Mom puts under the Christmas tree," Bradley said.

"Guys, what if they know about Lucy's plan?" Nate asked. "What if they're planning to capture us?"

"They're not getting me again!" Brian said. "I'm hiding!" He tore up the stairs.

"Let's barricade ourselves in our room," Bradley said.

He and Lucy and Nate followed Brian. They found him under his bed.

Bradley got down on his hands and knees. "Bri, come on out," he said. "We locked the bedroom door. We can move the dresser in front of it."

"I'm staying here till Mom and Dad get home," Brian said.

Nate knelt down, too. "The first place the aliens will look is under your bed," he said.

They heard Brian sigh. "Maybe it is a dream," he said. "And we're all in it."

Bradley reached under the bed and pinched his brother.

"Hey, what's that for?" Brian yelled.

"See, you're awake," Bradley said. "It's not a dream. Come on out, Bri. We need you to help us move the furniture."

Brian slid out from under the bed. His jeans and shirt were covered with dust.

"Hey, what's that?" Lucy asked. She was pointing at Pal's rubber hot dog on top of Brian's bed.

"It's Pal's toy hot dog," Brian said. "He must have left it there."

"But he took it outside when we were eating breakfast," Lucy said. "I saw him. I remember thinking he'd lose it in the snow."

Nate picked up the dog toy. "Does Pal have two rubber hot dogs?" he asked.

"Nope, only one," Bradley said.

"Then how did it get up here in your bedroom?" Lucy asked.

The four kids stared at each other.

Bradley looked up at the ceiling. "Oh no," he whispered.

Then he put his fingers to his lips. He pointed up. There was a heat vent in the ceiling.

Bradley grabbed a paper and pencil. He scribbled a note and held it up.

The note said:

Don't say anything.
They are listening!
Follow me!

9
Aliens in the Attic

Bradley dragged the other kids into the hallway.

He closed the bedroom door quietly.

He motioned for them all to follow him into the bathroom.

He shut that door, too.

"What's going on?" Brian asked.

"The aliens are hiding in the attic!" Bradley said. "They have Pal up there!"

"How do you know?" Lucy asked.

"Because Pal must have dropped his hot dog down through the ceiling heat vent," Bradley said. "It landed on Brian's bed."

"Oh my gosh!" Brian said. "Bradley's right! You know that red Christmas thing they threw over my head? Mom stores all the Christmas stuff in the attic!"

The four kids looked up at the bathroom ceiling.

"Do you think they can hear us?" asked Lucy.

"There's no vent in here," Bradley said.

"We don't even know if aliens have ears," Nate said.

Everyone just looked at him.

"Well, maybe they don't," insisted Nate.

"Guys, we need to focus!" Lucy said. "What if we write them a note telling them we want to swap for our families?"

"But the creepos in the attic don't

have our families," Brian reminded them all. "Dink, Josh, and Ruth Rose called us from a spaceship."

"Yeah, but maybe the guys in the attic can beam our message to the spaceship," Bradley said. "Write the note, Lucy."

Lucy dashed out of the bathroom. She was back in two minutes with paper and a pencil. "I locked the attic door," she said.

Lucy wrote in her best printing:

Dear space people,

We have you surrounded. Please give us back Polly, Pal, Dink, Josh, and Ruth Rose. If you do, we will let you go.

Your Earth friends,

Lucy, Nate, Brian, and Bradley

She showed the other kids the note.

"'We will let you go'?" Brian said. "We don't have them. They have us!"

"Well, maybe they don't know that," Lucy said.

Nate took the note from Lucy. "'Your Earth friends'?" he read. "Lucy, these guys are kidnappers from outer space! They're our enemies!"

"Well, it doesn't hurt to be nice," Lucy said.

"What if they can't read English?" Nate asked.

"Spaceships go everywhere," Lucy answered. "Aliens must know a bunch of languages."

Nate grinned and started to giggle. Bradley slapped his hand over his friend's mouth.

"Hey, wait a second," Brian said. "Why did the spaceship take off and leave two of their guys here?"

"Maybe so no one would see the ship," Bradley said. "It's probably just riding around up there, watching our house."

"Yeah, and they left their guys here to kidnap us," Nate said. "Then they'd signal the spaceship to come back and pick us up."

"Guys, I just thought of something else," Brian said. "What if it's not just us? What if the aliens grabbed a lot of people, not just our families? They could have taken people from all over Green Lawn. That spaceship could be filled with our neighbors!"

"Nah, we'd have heard about it on TV," Bradley said.

"Brad, we haven't even turned the TV on yet this morning," Brian said. "For all we know, the whole town has disappeared. We could be the only ones left!"

10
Mop Swap

"Don't panic," Lucy said. "Let's just give the aliens the note and see what happens."

"Not me!" Brian said. "I can still feel their yucky fingers all over me!"

Lucy folded the note neatly in half. "I'll do it," she said.

"What, you're just gonna open the attic door and walk up there?" Nate asked. "What if they keep you, too?"

"I'm not afraid of aliens!" Lucy said. "I'll just . . . I don't have a good idea."

Bradley reached behind the door for a mop. "I do," he said. "We can stick the note up through the ceiling vent on this."

"Brad, the ceiling is too high," Brian said.

"Lucy can stand on my bed," Bradley told his brother.

The kids trooped back to the bedroom.

Bradley gave Lucy some tape.

Lucy stuck the note to the end of the mop. Then she stood on the bed. The vent was right over her head.

"Ready?" Lucy whispered.

The three boys looked up and nodded. Lucy poked the mop handle through one of the holes in the vent.

She held it there.

Lucy looked down at the three boys with big eyes. "I feel something," she whispered.

They all heard a sound. It was the tape being removed from the handle.

Lucy lowered the mop.

The note was gone!

"Now what?" Nate asked.

"I don't know," Lucy said. "I guess we—"

Suddenly they heard loud thumping noises over their heads. Then they heard screeching, like fingernails on a blackboard.

"Run for your life!" Brian yelled. "They're mad at us!" He dove back under his bed.

Nate charged into the closet and slammed the door.

Lucy and Bradley stayed where they were, looking up.

The noises from above their heads stopped. Tiny pieces of paper fell from the vent like snowflakes. They landed on Lucy and Bradley.

Lucy grabbed some of the pieces. "It's my note!" she said.

"They tore it up," Bradley said.

Brian poked his head out from under the bed. "I guess that means they don't want to swap," he said.

Bradley opened his closet door. "Come on out, Nate," he said.

"Now I'm getting mad!" Lucy said. "That was totally rude!"

"Guys, my parents will be home pretty soon," Brian said. "How do we tell them that Dink, Josh, and Ruth Rose have been kidnapped by aliens?"

"Don't forget Polly and Pal," Nate added.

"I think it's time for a new plan," Bradley said.

11
Calling the Cops

Bradley put his finger to his lips and pointed toward the ceiling. He led the other kids into the hallway. They walked down to the kitchen.

"What's the new plan?" Lucy asked.

"We have to call Officer Fallon," Bradley said.

"Who's he?" asked Lucy.

"The chief of police," Nate told her.

"Bradley, Officer Fallon will think you're joking," Brian said. "When you say aliens, he'll just laugh!"

"How do you know?" Bradley asked. "A lot of grown-ups believe in aliens. It says so in my book."

"Okay," Brian said. "But *you're* talking to him, not me."

Bradley looked up the phone number and dialed. "Officer Fallon?" he said. "This is Bradley Pinto."

Then Bradley told Officer Fallon the whole story.

"Yes, sir, we will," Bradley said after listening for a minute.

He hung up the phone.

"What did he say?" Lucy asked.

"Did he believe you?" Brian asked.

"I don't know," Bradley said. "He said to keep the attic door locked and wait till he gets here."

The four kids sat at the kitchen table.

"Some of that cake would be nice," Nate commented.

"Forget it," Brian muttered.

Two minutes later they heard a siren.

Nate peeked out the window.

"The cops are here!" he said.

The kids grabbed their coats and ran outside. They almost bumped into Officer Fallon and Officer Keene.

"Have Josh and the others shown up yet?" Officer Keene asked the kids.

They all shook their heads.

Just then a fire engine roared into the yard. There were three firefighters in rubber suits and hard hats.

"Hey, Chief!" the man driving the engine yelled at Officer Fallon. "Where do you want the ladder?"

Officer Fallon looked at the twins. "Which one of you is Bradley?"

"I am," Bradley said. "That's Brian."

"I can never tell you two apart," Officer Fallon said.

"I have a tooth missing," Brian said. He proudly showed off his gap.

"Bradley, where's the attic window?" Officer Fallon asked.

Bradley pointed to the top window in the house. "That one," he said.

"Put the ladder there," Officer Fallon told the firefighter.

"Got it!" the man said. He backed the fire engine closer to the house. The ladder began rising until the top was right outside the attic window.

"Incoming car, Chief," said Officer Keene.

Brian and Bradley's parents pulled into the yard.

"It's Mom and Dad!" yelled Brian.

The twins' parents leaped out of their truck.

"What's happening?" their dad asked.

"Is the house on fire?" their mom cried.

One of the firefighters had climbed up the ladder. "Hey, Chief," he yelled down. "Should I smash this window?"

"No!" Officer Fallon yelled.

"What have you kids been up to?" the twins' father asked.

"There are aliens hiding in the attic," Nate said, grinning.

"Is this a joke?" the twins' mother asked. She looked around. "And where are the big kids?"

"It's not a joke, Mom," Bradley said. "I told you about the aliens, remember?"

Bradley's mother looked at him. "I know you did, hon," she said. "But I thought you were kidding around."

"Well, I wasn't!" Bradley said. "A spaceship landed in our yard last night, and they stole Josh and Dink and Ruth Rose!"

Bradley's parents looked at each other.

"And they took Polly and Pal," Nate chirped. "They're gonna eat 'em!"

Just then Officer Fallon walked over.

"Officer Fallon, what exactly is going on?" Bradley's father asked.

"I got a call from Bradley here, saying

the older kids—and your pets—had disappeared," Officer Fallon told Mr. and Mrs. Pinto. "Bradley told me he and his friends actually saw some aliens."

"One was green and one was yellow!" Bradley said. "They were peeking in the kitchen windows!"

"Great," his dad muttered. "I go to Ellie's Diner for breakfast and my family goes crazy!" He glared at his twin sons. "If this is some joke, you two are grounded. Forever!"

"Can we please go inside?" the twins' mother said. "The neighbors will think Green Lawn is being attacked!"

"It is, Mom!" Bradley said. "I even got a phone call from Josh in outer space!"

"Besides, we don't have any neighbors," Brian added.

"INSIDE!" his mother shouted. She marched up the back steps.

12
Aliens Appear

Everyone crowded into the kitchen.

"Who wants to tell us what's going on?" the boys' father asked.

Brian pointed at his brother. "Him. He started it all!"

"I did not!" Bradley said. "I know what we saw last night!"

"And what *did* you see, hon?" his mother asked.

"Lights from a spaceship," Bradley said. "I think."

"And then what happened?" Bradley's father asked.

Bradley and the other kids told the whole story. They tried not to leave anything out.

They told about:
the circle in the snow
and the footprints
and the printout from Josh's
    computer
and the faces in the window
and the noises in the attic
and the phone calls from space
and the rubber hot dog on the bed
and the ripped-up note.

When the story was over, the boys' parents and the officers had their mouths open.

Finally, Mrs. Pinto stood up. "Officer Fallon, will you please go into my attic and get those aliens?" she asked.

"Yes, ma'am!" Officer Fallon said. "You're backup, Officer Keene."

"Yes, sir!" Officer Keene said.

"What should we do?" Bradley asked.

"Just sit and wait," his mother said. "This should be very interesting."

"You might think about your punishment if this is all a prank," his father said.

"But, Dad, we all saw the aliens!" Bradley said.

Just then Officer Fallon entered the room. He was carrying a green alien in his two large hands.

Only it wasn't a real alien. It was a green sweater stuffed with newspapers. Painted toilet paper tubes were the arms and legs. Macaroni was glued on to look like teeth. A long string dangled from around its neck.

Officer Keene was right behind, holding the yellow alien.

"Hey, that's my very favorite golf sweater!" Bradley's father said.

"We found something else up there," Officer Fallon said.

He stepped aside. Dink, Josh, and
Ruth Rose stood behind him. Their faces
were red. Pal sat at Josh's feet, smiling at
all the people.

"Hey, you're supposed to be in a
spaceship!" Nate yelled.

"No, you're supposed to be in charge of the younger kids," the boys' father said. He gave Josh a stern look.

"We were in charge," Josh said. "Sort of. I mean, we were in the attic."

"You were up there the whole time?" Bradley said.

"We can explain," Josh said.

"I can hardly wait," his father said. He crossed his arms.

"Excuse me, but I think we'll leave you folks now," Officer Fallon said. "I'll tell the firefighters to take off, too."

"Right behind you," Officer Keene said.

"Thank you both," the boys' mother told the officers. She turned to the older kids again. "We're listening."

"It all started when Nate sent those postcards to Dink, Josh, and me," Ruth Rose said.

"What postcards?" Mr. Pinto asked.

"It was just a joke," Nate said. "The cards said they had won a million dollars in a contest."

"I decided to get back at him," Josh said.

"We all did," Dink said.

"I read Bradley's book about UFOs," Josh continued. "That's where I got the idea to pretend we were abducted by aliens."

"It was my idea to get Lucky O'Leary to help," Dink added. "He drove his snowmobile over last night to make the circle in the snow."

"I knew I saw moving lights!" Bradley said, beaming.

"Dink and Ruth Rose hid in the barn," Josh said. "They dangled those make-believe aliens out the window. I lit them up with a spotlight from the attic. Then I pounded on the floor to wake up the twins."

"And hiding Polly in our garage was my idea," Ruth Rose said.

"We carved potatoes to make those little footprints in the snow," Dink added.

"What about that paper we read from your computer?" Brian asked.

Josh grinned. "I wrote it myself."

"We knew all the parents were meeting for breakfast, so we planned it for today," Ruth Rose said.

The table grew silent.

"This calls for punishment," the boys' mother said.

13
See the Real, Live Aliens!

"And I think the younger kids should choose the punishment for the older kids," Mr. Pinto added.

"Yes!" Brian shouted.

"No fair!" Josh argued. "They'll make us stay in our rooms for ten years with no food!"

"No, they won't," Josh's mother said. She looked at the four younger kids. "You'll be fair, right?"

The four kids nodded.

"Okay, then go into the other room and decide," she said.

The twins and Nate and Lucy scooted into the living room.

"I go first because I'm oldest!" Brian said. "I say we make them walk around Green Lawn in their underwear."

Nate nearly fell over laughing. "I've got a better one!" he said. "How about if we make them clean our rooms and make us snacks every day for a year?"

"Those are both too mean," Lucy said. "Besides, I don't want them in my room poking around in my stuff."

"Lucy's right," Bradley said.

"So what should the punishment be?" Brian asked.

Bradley grinned. "What if we make them dress up as aliens and sit in Ellie's Diner?" he asked.

The other three kids stared at Bradley.

"And we get to dress them," Bradley added.

Then they did a four-kid high five.

. . .

The next Saturday morning Ellie's Diner was more crowded than usual. In fact, there was a line waiting to get in.

Bradley and Brian, Nate, and Lucy stood outside holding a banner.

The sign said: MEET REAL, LIVE SPACE ALIENS INSIDE!

Officer Fallon stopped to read the banner.

"What's this about?" he asked. "Another January joke?"

"No, this time they're real!" Nate said.

Officer Fallon grinned, shook his head, and walked inside.

The kids rolled up the banner and followed Officer Fallon.

Dink, Josh, and Ruth Rose were sitting together in a booth. Their skin was green. They had fat bellies. Tinfoil antennas sprouted from their heads.

Each kid had a pair of goggly yellow eyes.

Officer Fallon walked up to the booth. He had a big smile on his face. "Gee, real, live space aliens," he said, pulling his notebook from his shirt pocket. "Do you sign autographs?"

"They're not allowed to talk!" Bradley said.

Josh reached out a green hand. His fingernails were purple.

Officer Fallon gave him the pad and a pencil.

Josh wrote: BUY US ICE CREAM, AND WE'LL SIGN ANYTHING!

Officer Fallon showed the note to the younger kids. "What do you think?" he asked.

"Sure," Bradley said. "Aliens like ice cream, too!"

If you like Calendar Mysteries, you might want to read A to Z Mysteries!

Help Dink, Josh, and Ruth Rose . . .

. . . solve mysteries from A to Z!

Track down all these books for a little mystery in your life!

**A to Z Mysteries®
by Ron Roy**

**Calendar Mysteries
by Ron Roy**

**Capital Mysteries
by Ron Roy**

Marion Dane Bauer
The Blue Ghost
The Green Ghost
The Red Ghost
The Secret of the Painted House

Polly Berrien Berends
The Case of the Elevator Duck

Éric Sanvoisin
The Ink Drinker

George Edward Stanley
Ghost Horse

Read all of KC and Marshall's adventures in Washington, D.C.!

Capital Mysteries

Turn the page for the first chapter of Brian, Bradley, Lucy, and Nate's next exciting mystery:

Calendar **Mysteries**

February Friend

With the younger siblings of the A to Z Mysteries® kids!

by Ron Roy

1
Secret Valentine

"I love Valentine's Day," Bradley Pinto told his twin brother. They were walking to school. Both boys had green ski caps pulled down over their red hair. They wore matching ski jackets.

"Why, because girls send you valentines?" Brian asked.

Bradley shook his head. "Nope. Because Mom always makes cupcakes!" He was carrying a box of them.

Bradley and Brian met their friends Nate Hathaway and Lucy Armstrong in front of their school. Nate had black hair like his older sister, Ruth Rose. Lucy's blond ponytail hung from under her fuzzy white hat.

Lucy was staying with her cousin Dink's family for one year. Dink was best friends with Ruth Rose and the twins' brother, Josh. Lucy's parents were in Arizona helping to build a school on a reservation.

Nate tapped the box Bradley was holding. "How many cupcakes did your mom make?" he asked. He rubbed his tummy.

"Twenty-four," Bradley said.

"Is that all?" Nate asked. "I could eat ten all by myself!"

"Dream on," Lucy said.

Nate had brought paper plates, napkins, and plastic forks. Lucy was carrying a bag of heart-shaped cookies.

Just then a loud bell clanged. The

four friends hurried into the school. A bunch of other kids were scurrying to their classrooms as well. A few parents came in carrying boxes. The janitor, Mr. Neater, was mopping up snow puddles.

The kids' first-grade teacher, Mr. Vooray, waited for them outside his classroom. The rest of the class was already in the room. Two of the kids were feeding Goldilocks, the hamster, and Yertle, the box turtle.

"Happy Valentine's Day," Mr. Vooray said. "Please put your goodies on the counter. And everyone hang up your coats."

Bradley, Nate, and Lucy carried the cupcakes, cookies, plates, and forks over to the counter. Bradley noticed other cupcakes, a plate of brownies, and a bowl of candy hearts.

A big red box sat on Mr. Vooray's desk. The box was decorated with paper hearts. All the kids knew it was filled with valentines. They had been making them all week.

"When can we open the box?" Samantha asked Mr. Vooray.

"As you know, today is a half day," Mr. Vooray said. "I think we should wait till just before we go home. Then we can pass out the valentines and eat all the treats you kids brought in."

The morning went quickly. The first graders did math problems. Then they wrote in their journals. When they were finished with that, they read in their library books.

Then Mr. Vooray read aloud from *Charlotte's Web*.

Suddenly Nate's tummy growled.

Mr. Vooray looked up. "I guess it's time to eat," he said with a smile.

Everyone jumped up and ran for the counter. Kids giggled and bumped into each other as they handed out paper plates, napkins, forks, and cups of juice. Then the kids who had brought food passed it out. Soon everyone was munching.

Bradley bit into a chocolate cupcake with pink frosting. He and his mom had frosted them early that morning.

"When can we get our valentines?" Joyce asked.

"Right now!" Mr. Vooray said. He pulled the lid off the red box and dumped a big pile of valentine cards on his desk. He picked Flo, Bradley, and Lucy to pass them out to the class.

"Hey, Mr. Vooray, here's one with no name on it," Bradley said. He held up the envelope. It was red and shaped like a heart.

Mr. Vooray grinned. "It's a mystery card," he said.

"Open it!" a bunch of kids yelled.

"Go ahead," said Mr. Vooray.

Bradley opened the envelope. He pulled out a heart-shaped card and showed the class. On the front was a picture of a bunny rabbit.

Bradley read what was written inside the card: "LOOK IN THE CLOSET."

Mr. Vooray walked over to the closet. He put his ear to the door. "I hear something," he whispered.